Naughtiest Stories

Naughtiest Stories

Compiled by Barbara Ireson
Illustrated by Tony Ross

RED FOX

A Red Fox Book

Published by Random House Children's Books
20 Vauxhall Bridge Road, London SW1V 2SA

A division of Random House UK Ltd

London Melbourne Sydney Auckland Johannesburg
and agencies throughout the world

3 5 7 9 10 8 6 4 2

Red Fox edition 1994

Printed and bound in Great Britain by
Cox & Wyman Ltd, Reading, Berkshire

RANDOM HOUSE UK Limited Reg. No. 954009

ISBN 0 09 929901 1

Contents

The Boy Who Wasn't Bad Enough

Lance Salway

A long time ago, in a far country, there lived a boy called Claud who was so bad that people both far and near had heard of his naughtiness. His mother and father loved him dearly, and so did his brothers and sisters, but even they became angry at the tricks he played on them and the mischief that he caused by his bad behaviour.

Once, when his grandmother came to stay, Claud put a big, fat frog in her bed. Once, when the teacher wasn't looking, he changed the hands on the school clock so that the children were sent home two hours early. And once, when Claud was feeling especially bad, he cut his mother's washing line so that the clean clothes fell into the mud, and he poured a bottle of ink over the head of his eldest sister, and he locked his two young brothers into a cupboard and threw the key down a well. And, as if that wasn't

1

bad enough, he climbed to the top of the tallest tree in the garden and tied his father's best shirt to the topmost branch so that it waved in the wind like a flag.

His parents and his brothers and sisters did all they could to stop Claud's mischief and to make him a better boy. They sent him to bed without any supper, but that didn't make any difference. They wouldn't let him go to the circus when it came to the town, but that didn't make any difference. They wouldn't let him go out to play with his friends, but that didn't make any difference either because Claud hadn't any friends. All the other boys and girls of the town were much too frightened to play with him and, in any case, their parents wouldn't let them. But Claud didn't mind. He liked to play tricks on people and he enjoyed being as bad as possible. And he laughed when his parents became cross or his brothers and sisters cried because he liked to see how angry they would get when he was naughty.

'What *are* we to do with you?' sighed his mother. 'We've tried everything we can think of to stop you being so naughty. And it hasn't made any difference at all.'

'But I enjoy being bad,' said Claud, and he pushed his youngest sister so hard that she fell on the floor with a thump.

Everybody in the town had heard of Claud's naughtiness, and it wasn't long before the news spread to the next town and the next until everyone had heard that Claud was the naughtiest boy in the land. The king and queen had heard of Claud's naughtiness. And even the Chief Witch, who was the oldest and the ugliest and the most wicked witch in the kingdom, had heard of him too.

One day, the Chief Witch came to visit Claud's parents. They were very frightened when they saw her but Claud was overjoyed, especially when she told him that if he promised to be very bad indeed she would allow him to ride on her broomstick.

'I believe your son is the naughtiest boy in the whole country,' she said to Claud's father.

'He is,' he replied, sadly.

'Good!' said the Witch. 'I would like him to join my school for bad children. We are always looking for clever children to train as witches and wizards. And the naughtier they are, the better.'

Claud was very pleased when he heard of the Witch's plan and he begged his parents to allow him to go to her school.

'At least we'd have some peace,' said his mother. 'Yes, you may as well go, if it will make you happy.'

'Oh, it will, it will!' shouted Claud, and he rushed upstairs to get ready for the journey. And so, a few days later, the Chief Witch called again on her broomstick to take Claud to her school. He said goodbye to his parents and his brothers and sisters and climbed on to the broomstick behind her. He couldn't wave to his family but he smiled happily at them as he flew away on the long journey to school, clutching the broomstick with one hand and holding his suitcase with the other.

Everybody was pleased to see him go. The people of the town were pleased. Claud's brothers and sisters were pleased.

'Now we can enjoy ourselves,' they said. 'Claud won't be here to play tricks on us now.'

Even his mother and father were pleased. 'He'll be happy with the Witch,' they said. 'He can be as bad as he likes now.'

But, as time passed, they found that they all missed Claud.

'It was much more fun when he was here,' complained his brothers and sisters. 'We never knew what would happen next.'

Claud's mother and father, too, began to wish that he had never gone away. Even though he was such a bad boy they loved him dearly and wished that they had never allowed the Chief Witch to take him to school. And the people of

the town wished that Claud would come back.

'There was never a dull moment when Claud was here,' they sighed. 'Now, nothing ever happens in our town.'

As the weeks passed, Claud's family missed him more and more.

'Perhaps he'll come back to visit us,' his mother said.

But the summer ended and autumn passed and then winter came but still there was no visit from Claud.

'He'll never come back,' said his father, sadly.

And then, on a cold night in the middle of winter, they heard a faint knock on the front door.

'I wonder who that can be,' said Claud's mother, as she went to open it. 'Why, it's Claud!' she cried. And it was. He stood shivering on the doorstep, looking very thin and miserable and cold.

'We're so glad you've come back,' said his father. 'Sit down and tell us what happened and why you've come back to us.'

'I wasn't bad enough,' Claud said, and burst into tears. And then, when he had been given something to eat and had warmed himself by the fire, he told his parents about the school and about the very wicked children who were there.

'They were even naughtier than I am,' he

said. 'They turned people into frogs. They turned *me* into a frog until the Witch told them to turn me back. They were much, much naughtier than me. And even though I tried very hard indeed I just couldn't be as bad as the others. And so the Witch said I was too good ever to become a wicked wizard and she sent me away.'

'Never mind,' said his parents. 'We're very pleased to see you. We've missed you.'

His brothers and sisters were overjoyed at Claud's return. They laughed when Claud filled their shoes with jam while they were asleep. And they laughed when Claud tied them all to a tree. They even laughed when he pushed them all into the goldfish pond.

'Good old Claud!' they shouted. 'We're glad you're back!'

His mother laughed when she found out he had put beetles into the tea caddy. And his father didn't seem to mind when Claud cut large holes in his newspaper.

'Claud's back and quite his old self again,' they said, and smiled at each other.

But soon Claud found that being naughty wasn't as much fun any more. 'Nobody seems to mind my tricks,' he complained, 'even the new ones I learned at the Witch's school. People laugh when I trip them up, or tie their shoelaces together, or put ants in their hair. Why can't they be as angry as they used to be?'

So, because being bad wasn't any fun any more, Claud decided to be good instead. Not *completely* good, of course. Every now and again he would throw mud at his brothers and once he even covered the cat with a mixture of shoe polish and marmalade. But people soon forgot that he was once the naughtiest boy in the whole country. And the Chief Witch was so disappointed in Claud that she didn't call again.

Playing With Cuthbert

René Goscinny

I wanted to go out and play with our gang, but Mum said no, nothing doing, she didn't care for the little boys I went around with, we were always up to something silly, and anyway I was invited to tea with Cuthbert, who was a nice little boy with such good manners, and it would be a very good thing if I tried to be more like him.

I wasn't mad keen to go to tea with Cuthbert, or try to be more like him. Cuthbert is top of the class and teacher's pet and a rotten sport but we can't thump him much because of his glasses. I'd rather have gone to the swimming pool with Alec and Geoffrey and Eddie and the rest, but there it was, Mum looked as if she wasn't standing for any nonsense, and anyway I always do what my mum says, especially when she looks as if she isn't standing for any nonsense.

Mum made me wash and comb my hair and told me to put on my blue sailor suit with the nice creases in the trousers, and my white silk shirt and spotted tie. I had to wear that lot for my cousin Angela's wedding, the time I was sick after the reception.

'And don't look like that!' said Mum. 'You'll have a very nice time playing with Cuthbert, I'm sure.'

Then we went out. I was scared stiff of meeting the gang. They'd have laughed like a drain to see me got up like that!

Cuthbert's mum opened the door. 'Oh, isn't he sweet!' she said, and she hugged me and then she called Cuthbert. 'Cuthbert! Come along. Here's your little friend Nicholas.' So Cuthbert came along, he was all dressed up too, with velvet trousers and white socks and funny shiny black sandals. We looked a pair of right Charlies, him and me.

Cuthbert didn't look all that pleased to see me either, he shook my hand and his hand was all limp. 'Well, I'll be off,' said Mum. 'I hope he'll behave, and I'll be back to pick him up at six.' And Cuthbert's mum said she was sure we'd play nicely and I'd be very good. Mum gave me a rather worried look and then she went away.

We had tea. That was OK, there was choc-

olate to drink and jam and cake and biscuits and we didn't put our elbows on the table. After tea Cuthbert's mum told us to go and have a nice game in Cuthbert's room.

Up in his room Cuthbert started by telling me I mustn't thump him because he wore glasses and if I did he'd start to shout and his mum would have me put in prison. I told him I'd just love to thump him, but I wasn't going to because I'd promised my mum to be good. Cuthbert seemed to like the sound of that, and he said right, we'd play. He got out heaps of books: geography books and science books and arithmetic books, and he said we could read and do some sums to pass the time. He told me he knew some brilliant problems about the water from taps running into a bath with the plug pulled out so the bath emptied at the same time as it was filling.

That didn't sound like a bad idea, and I asked Cuthbert if I could see his bath because it might be fun. Cuthbert looked at me, took off his glasses, wiped them, thought a minute and then told me to come with him.

There was a big bath in the bathroom and I said why didn't we fill it and sail boats on it? Cuthbert said he'd never thought of that, but it was quite a good idea. The bath didn't take long to fill right up to the top (we put the plug in, not like the problem). But then we were stuck because Cuthbert didn't have any boats to sail in it. He explained that he didn't have many toys at all, he mostly had books. But luckily I can make paper boats and we took some pages out of his arithmetic book. Of course we tried to be careful so that Cuthbert could stick the pages back in the book afterwards, because it's very naughty to harm a book, a tree or a poor dumb animal.

We had a really great time. Cuthbert swished his arm about in the water to make waves. It was a pity he didn't roll up his shirt-sleeves first, and he didn't take off the watch he got for coming first in the last history test we had and now it says twenty past four all the time. After a bit longer, I don't know just how much longer because of the watch not working, we'd had enough of playing boats. Anyway there was water all over the place and we didn't want to make too much mess because there were muddy puddles on the floor and Cuthbert's sandals weren't as shiny as they used to be.

We went back to Cuthbert's room and he showed me his globe, which is a big metal ball on a stand with seas and continents and things on it. Cuthbert explained that it was for learning geography and finding where the different countries were. I knew that already, there's a globe like that at school and our teacher showed us how it works. Cuthbert told me you could unscrew his globe, and then it was like a big ball. I think it was me that got the idea of playing ball with it, only that turned out not to be such a very good idea after all. We did have some fun throwing and catching the globe, but Cuthbert had taken off his glasses so as not to risk breaking them, and he doesn't see very well without his glasses, so he missed the globe and the part with Australia on it hit his mirror and the mirror got broken. Cuthbert put his glasses on again to see what had happened and he was very upset. We put the globe back on its stand and decided to be more careful in case our mums weren't too pleased.

So we looked for something else to do, and Cuthbert told me his dad had given him a chemistry set to help him with science. He showed me the chemistry set; it's brilliant. It's a big box full of tubes and funny round bottles and little flasks full of things all different colours, and a spirit burner too. Cuthbert told me you could do some very instructive experiments with this chemistry set.

He started pouring little bits of powder and liquid into the tubes and they changed colour and went red or blue and now and then there was a puff of white smoke. It was ever so instructive. I told Cuthbert we ought to try something even more instructive, and he agreed. We took the biggest bottle and tipped all the powders and liquids into it and then we got the spirit burner and heated up the bottle. It was OK to start with; the stuff began frothing up, and then there was some very black smoke. The trouble was the smoke didn't smell too good and it made everything very dirty. When the bottle burst we had to stop the experiment.

Cuthbert started howling that he couldn't see any more, but luckily it was only because the lenses of his glasses were all black, and while he wiped them I opened the window, because the

smoke was making us cough. And the froth was
making funny noises on the carpet, like boiling
water, and the walls were all black and we
weren't terribly clean ourselves.

Then Cuthbert's mum came in. For a moment
she didn't say anything at all, just opened her
eyes and her mouth very wide, and then she
started to shout, she took off Cuthbert's glasses
and she slapped him, and then she led us off to
the bathroom to get washed. When Cuthbert's

mum saw the bathroom she wasn't too pleased about that either.

Cuthbert was hanging on to his glasses for dear life, so as not to get slapped again. Cuthbert's mum went off telling me she was going to ring my mother and ask her to come and fetch me immediately and she'd never seen anything like it in all her born days and it was absolutely incredible.

Mum did come to fetch me pretty soon, and I was pleased because I wasn't having so much fun at Cuthbert's house any more, not with his mum carrying on like that. Mum took me home, telling me all the way she supposed I was proud of myself and I wouldn't have any pudding this evening. I must say, that was fair enough, because we did do one or two daft things at Cuthbert's. And actually Mum was right, as usual: I *did* have a nice time playing with Cuthbert. I'd have liked to go and see him again, but it seems that Cuthbert's mum doesn't want him to be friends with me.

Honestly, mothers! I do wish they could make up their minds, you just don't know *who* to play with!

The Crooked Little Finger

Philippa Pearce

One morning Judy woke up with a funny feeling in her little finger. It didn't exactly hurt; but it was beginning to ache and it was beginning to itch. It felt wrong. She held it straight out, and it still felt wrong. She curved it in on itself, with all the other fingers, and it still felt wrong.

In the end, she got dressed and went down to breakfast, holding that little finger straight up in the air, quite separately.

She sat down to breakfast, and said to her mother and her father and to her big brother, David, and her young sister, Daisy: 'My little finger's gone wrong.'

David asked: 'What have you done to it?'

'Nothing,' said Judy. 'I just woke up this morning and it somehow felt wrong.'

Her mother said: 'I expect you'll wake up tomorrow morning and it'll somehow feel right.'

'What about today though?' asked Judy; but

her mother wasn't listening any more.

Her father said: 'You haven't broken a bone in your little finger, have you, Judy? Can you bend it? Can you crook it – like this – as though you were beckoning with it?'

'Yes,' said Judy; and then 'Ooooow!'

'Did it hurt, then?' said her mother, suddenly listening again, and anxious.

'No,' said Judy. 'It didn't hurt at all when I crooked it. But it felt *very* funny. It felt wrong. I didn't like it.'

David said: 'I'm tired of Judy's little finger'; and their mother said: 'Forget your little finger, Judy, and get on with your breakfast.'

So Judy stopped talking about her little finger, but she couldn't forget it. It felt so odd. She tried crooking it again, and discovered that it wanted to crook itself. That was what it had been aching to do and itching to do.

She crooked it while she poured milk on her cereal and then waited for David to finish with the sugar.

Suddenly –

'Hey!' David cried angrily. 'Don't *do* that, Judy!'

'What is it now?' exclaimed their mother, startled.

'She snatched the sugar from under my nose, just when I was helping myself.' He was still holding the sugar spoon in the air.

'I didn't!' said Judy.

'You did!' said David. 'How else did the sugar get from me to you like that?'

'I crooked my little finger at it,' said Judy.

David said: 'What rubbish!'; and their mother said: 'Pass the sugar back to David at once, Judy.'

Their father said nothing, but stared at Judy's little finger; and Daisy said: 'The sugar went quick through the air. I saw it.' But nobody paid any attention to Daisy, of course.

Judy began to say: 'My little finger – '

But her mother interrupted her: 'Judy, we don't want to hear any more at all about that little finger. There's nothing wrong with it.'

So Judy said no more at all about her little finger; but it went on feeling very wrong.

Her father was the first to go, off to work. He kissed his wife goodbye, and his baby daughter, Daisy. He said, 'Be a good boy!' to David, and he said, 'Be a good girl!' to Judy. Then he stopped and kissed Judy, which he didn't usually do in the morning rush, and he whispered in her ear: 'Watch out for that little finger of yours that wants to be crooked!'

Then he went off to work; and, a little later, Judy and David went off to school.

And Judy's little finger still felt wrong, aching

and itching in its strange way.

Judy sat in her usual place in the classroom, listening to Mrs Potter reading a story aloud. While she listened, Judy looked round the classroom, and caught sight of an india-rubber she had often seen before and wished was hers. The india-rubber was shaped and coloured just like a perfect little pink pig with a roving eye. It belonged to a boy called Simon, whom she didn't know very well. Even if they had known each other very well indeed, he probably wouldn't have wanted to give Judy his perfect pink pig india-rubber.

As it was, Judy just stared at the india-rubber and longed to have it. While she longed, her

little finger began to ache very much indeed and
to itch very much indeed. It ached and itched
to be allowed to crook itself, to beckon.

In the end Judy crooked her little finger.

Then there was a tiny sound like a puff of
breath, and something came sailing through the
air from Simon's table to Judy's table, and it
landed with a little *flop!* just by Judy's hand.
And Mrs Potter had stopped reading the story,
and was crying: 'Whatever are you doing, Simon
Smith, to be throwing india-rubbers about? We
don't throw india-rubbers about in this classroom!'

'I didn't throw my india-rubber!' said Simon.

He was very much flustered.

21

'Then how does it happen to be here?' Mrs Potter had come over to Judy's table to pick up the india-rubber. She turned it over, and there was SIMON SMITH written in ink on the underside.

Simon said nothing; and, of course, Judy said nothing; and Mrs Potter said: 'We *never* throw india-rubbers about in this classroom, Simon. I shall put this india-rubber up on my desk, and there it stays until the dinner-break.'

But it didn't stay there – oh, no! Judy waited and waited until no one in the classroom – no one at all – was looking; and then she crooked her little finger, and the india-rubber came sailing through the air again – *flop!* on to her table, just beside her. This time Judy picked it up very quickly and quietly and put it into her pocket.

At the end of the morning, Simon went up to Mrs Potter's desk to get his india-rubber back again; and it wasn't there. He searched round about, and so did Mrs Potter, but they couldn't find the india-rubber. In the end, Mrs Potter was bothered and cross, and Simon was crying. They had no idea where the india-rubber could have got to.

But Judy knew exactly where it was.

Now Judy knew what her little finger could do – what it ached and itched to be allowed to do. But she didn't want anyone else to know what it could do. That would have spoilt everything. She would have had to return Simon's pink pig india-rubber and anything else her little finger crooked itself to get.

So she was very, very careful. At dinner time she managed to crook her little finger at a second helping of syrup pudding, when no one was looking; and she got it, and ate it. Later on, she crooked her little finger at the prettiest seashell on the nature table, and no one saw it come through the air to her; and she put it into her pocket with the pink pig india-rubber. Later still, she crooked her finger at another girl's hair-ribbon, that was hanging loose, and at a useful two-coloured pencil. By the end of the school day, the pocket with the pink pig india-rubber was crammed full of things which did not belong to Judy but which had come to her when she crooked her little finger.

And what did Judy feel like? Right in the middle of her – in her stomach – she felt a heaviness, because she had eaten too much syrup pudding.

In her head, at the very top of her head, there was a fizziness of airy excitement that made her feel almost giddy.

And somewhere between the top of her head and her stomach she felt uncomfortable. She wanted to think about all the things hidden in her pocket, and to enjoy the thought; but, on the other hand, she didn't want to think about them at all. Especially she didn't want to think about Simon Smith crying and crying for his pink pig india-rubber. The wanting to think and the *not* wanting to think made her feel very uncomfortable indeed.

When school was over, Judy went home with her brother David, as usual. They were passing the sweet shop, not far from their home, when Judy said: 'I'd like some chocolate, or some toffees.'

'You haven't any money to buy chocolate or toffees,' said David. 'Nor have I. Come on, Judy.'

Judy said: 'Daisy once went in there, and the shopman gave her a toffee. She hadn't any money, and he *gave* her a toffee.'

'That's because she was so little – a baby, really,' said David. 'He wouldn't give you a toffee, if you hadn't money to buy it.'

'It's not fair,' said Judy. And her little finger felt as if it agreed with her: it ached and it itched, and it longed to crook itself. But Judy wouldn't let it – yet. She and David passed the sweet shop and went home to tea.

After tea, it grew dark outside. Indoors everyone was busy, except for Judy. Her mother was bathing Daisy and putting her to bed; her father was mending something; David was making an aeroplane out of numbered parts. Nobody was noticing Judy, so she slipped out of the house and went along the street to the sweet shop.

It was quite dark by now, except for the street-lamps. All the shops were shut; there was nobody about. Judy would have been frightened to be out alone, after dark, without anyone's knowing, but her little finger ached and her little finger itched, and she could think of nothing else.

She reached the sweet shop, and looked in through the window. There were pretty tins of toffee and chocolate boxes tied with bright ribbon on display in the window. She peered beyond them, to the back of the shop, where she could just see the bars of chocolate stacked like bricks and the rows of big jars of boiled sweets and the packets and cartons and tubes of sweets and toffees and chocolates and other delightful things that she could only guess at in the dimness of the inside of the shop.

And Judy crooked her little finger.

She held her little finger crooked, and she saw the bars of chocolate and the jars of boiled sweets and all the other things beginning to move from the back of the shop towards the front, towards the window. Soon the window was crowded close with sweets of all kinds pressing against the glass, as though they had come to stare at her and at her crooked little finger. Judy backed away from the shop window, to the other side of the street; but she still held her little finger crooked, and all the things in the sweet shop pressed up against the window, and pressed and crowded and pressed and pressed, harder and harder, against the glass of the shop window, until –

CRACK!

The window shattered, and everything in it came flying out towards Judy as she stood there with her little finger crooked.

She was so frightened that she turned and ran for home as fast as she could, and behind her she heard a hundred thousand things from the sweet shop come skittering and skidding and bumping and thumping along the pavement after her.

She ran and she ran and she reached her front gate and then her front door and she ran in through the front door and slammed it shut behind her, and heard all the things that had been chasing her come rattling and banging against the front door, and then fall to the ground.

Then she found that she had uncrooked her little finger.

Although she was safe now, Judy ran upstairs to her bedroom and flung herself upon her bed and cried. As she lay there, crying, she held her little finger out straight in front of her, and said to it: 'I hate you – I HATE you!'

From her bed, she began to hear shouts and cries and the sound of running feet in the street outside, and her father's voice, and then her mother's, as they went out to see what had happened. There were people talking and talking, their voices high and loud with excitement and amazement. Later, there was the sound of a police car coming, and more talk.

But, in the end, the noise and the excitement

died away, and at last everything was quiet. Then she heard footsteps on the stairs, and her bedroom door opened, and her father's voice said: 'Are you there, Judy?'

'Yes.'

He came in and sat down on her bed. He said that her mother was settling Daisy, so he had come to tell her what had been happening. He said there had been a smash-and-grab raid at the sweet shop. There must have been a whole gang of raiders, and they had got clean away: no one had seen them. But the gang had had to dump their loot in their hurry to escape. They had thrown it all – chocolates and toffees and sweets and everything – into the first convenient front garden. Judy's father said that the stuff had all been flung into their own front garden and against their own front door.

As she listened, Judy wept and wept. Her father did not ask her why she was crying; but at last he said: 'How is that little finger?'

Judy said: 'I hate it!'

'I daresay,' said her father. 'But does it ache and itch any more?'

Judy thought a moment. 'No,' she said, 'it doesn't.' She stopped crying.

'Judy,' said her father, 'if it ever starts aching and itching again, *don't crook it*.'

'I won't,' said Judy. 'I never will again. Never.

Ever.'

The next day Judy went early to school, even before David. When she got into the classroom, only Mrs Potter was there, at the teacher's desk.

Judy went straight to the teacher's desk and brought out from her pocket the pink pig india-rubber and the shell and the hair-ribbon and the two-colour pencil and all the other things. She put them on Mrs Potter's desk, and Mrs Potter looked at them, and said nothing.

Judy said: 'I'm sorry. I'm really and truly sorry. And my father says to tell you that I had a crooked little finger yesterday. But it won't crook itself again, ever. I shan't let it.'

'I've heard of crooked little fingers,' said Mrs Potter. 'In the circumstances, Judy, we'll say no more.'

And Judy's little finger never crooked itself again, ever.

Licked

Paul Jennings

Tomorrow when Dad calms down I'll own up. Tell him the truth. He might laugh. He might cry. He might strangle me. But I have to put him out of his misery.

I like my dad. He takes me fishing. He gives me arm wrestles in front of the fire on cold nights. He plays Scrabble instead of watching the news. He tries practical jokes on me. And he keeps his promises. Always.

But he has two faults. Bad faults. One is to do with flies. He can't stand them. If there's a fly in the room he has to kill it. He won't use fly spray because of the ozone layer so he chases them with a fly swat. He races around the house swiping and swatting like a mad thing. He won't stop until the fly is flat. Squashed. Squished – sometimes still squirming on the end of the fly swat.

He's a dead-eye shot. He hardly ever misses.

30

When his old fly swat was almost worn out I bought him a nice new yellow one for his birthday. It wasn't yellow for long. It soon had bits of fly smeared all over it.

It's funny the different colours that squashed flies have inside them. Mostly it is black or brown. But often there are streaks of runny red stuff and sometimes bits of blue. The wings flash like diamonds if you hold them up to the light. But mostly the wings fall off unless they are stuck to the swat with a bit of squashed innards.

Chasing flies is Dad's first fault. His second one is table manners. He is mad about manners.

And it is always my manners that are the matter.

'Andrew,' he says. 'Don't put your elbows on the table.'

'Don't talk with your mouth full.'

'Don't lick your fingers.'

'Don't dunk your biscuit in the coffee.'

This is the way he goes on every meal time. He has a thing about flies and a thing about manners.

Anyway, to get back to the story. One day Dad is peeling the potatoes for tea. I am looking for my fifty cents that rolled under the table about a week ago. Mum is cutting up the cabbage and talking to Dad. They do not know that

I am there. It is a very important meal because Dad's boss, Mr Spinks, is coming for tea. Dad never stops going on about my manners when someone comes for tea.

'You should stop picking on Andrew at tea time,' says Mum.

'I don't,' says Dad.

'Yes you do,' says Mum. 'It's always "don't do this, don't do that". You'll give the boy a complex.'

I have never heard of a complex before but I guess that it is something awful like pimples.

'Tonight,' says Mum, 'I want you to go for the whole meal without telling Andrew off once.'

'Easy,' says Dad.

'Try hard,' says Mum. 'Promise me that you won't get cross with him.'

Dad looks at her for a long time. 'OK,' he says. 'It's a deal. I won't say one thing about his manners. But you're not allowed to either. What's good for me is good for you.'

'Shake,' says Mum. They shake hands and laugh.

I find the fifty cents and sneak out. I take a walk down the street to spend it before tea. Dad has promised not to tell me off at tea time. I think about how I can make him crack. It should be easy. I will slurp my soup. He hates that. He will tell me off. He might even yell. I just know that he can't go for the whole meal without going crook. 'This is going to be fun,' I say to myself.

That night Mum sets the table with the new tablecloth. And the best knives and forks. And the plates that I am not allowed to touch. She puts out serviettes in little rings. All of this means that it is an important meal. We don't usually use serviettes.

Mr Spinks comes in his best suit. He wears gold glasses and he frowns a lot. I can tell that he doesn't like children. You can always tell when adults don't like kids. They smile at you with their lips but not with their eyes.

Anyway, we sit down to tea. I put my secret weapon on the floor under the table. I'm sure that I can make Dad crack without using it. But it is there if all else fails.

The first course is soup and bread rolls. I make loud slurping noises with the soup. No one says anything about it. I make the slurping noises longer and louder. They go on and on and on. It sounds like someone has pulled the plug out of the bath. Dad clears his throat but doesn't say anything.

I try something different. I dip my bread in the soup and make it soggy. Then I hold it high above my head and drop it down into my mouth. I catch it with a loud slopping noise. I try again with an even bigger bit. This time I miss my mouth and the bit of soupy bread hits me in the eye.

Nothing is said. Dad looks at me. Mum looks at me. Mr Spinks tries not to look at me. They are talking about how Dad might get a promotion at work. They are pretending that I am not revolting.

The next course is chicken. Dad will crack over the chicken. He'll say something. He hates me picking up the bones.

The chicken is served. 'I've got the chicken's bottom,' I say in a loud voice.

Dad glares at me but he doesn't answer. I pick up the chicken and start stuffing it into my mouth with my fingers. I grab a roast potato and break it in half. I dip my fingers into the margarine and put some on the potato. It runs all over the place.

I have never seen anyone look as mad as the way Dad looks at me. He glares. He stares. He clears his throat. But still he doesn't crack. What a man. Nothing can make him break his promise.

I snap a chicken bone in half and suck out the middle. It is hollow and I can see right through it. I suck and slurp and swallow. Dad is going red in the face. Little veins are standing out on his nose. But still he does not crack.

The last course is baked apple and custard. I will get him with that. Mr Spinks has stopped talking about Dad's promotion. He is discussing something about discipline. About setting limits. About insisting on standards. Something like that. I put the hollow bone into the custard and use it like a straw. I suck the custard up the hollow chicken bone.

Dad clears his throat. He is very red in the face. 'Andrew,' he says.

He is going to crack. I have won.

'Yes,' I say through a mouth full of custard.

'Nothing,' he mumbles.

Dad is terrific. He is under enormous pressure but still he keeps his cool. There is only one thing left to do. I take out my secret weapon.

I place the yellow fly swat on the table next to my knife.

Everyone looks at it lying there on the white tablecloth. They stare and stare and stare. But nothing is said.

I pick up the fly swat and start to lick it. I lick it like an ice cream. A bit of chewy, brown goo comes off on my tongue. I swallow it quickly. Then I crunch a bit of crispy, black stuff.

Mr Spinks rushes out to the kitchen. I can hear him being sick in the kitchen sink.

Dad stands up. It is too much for him. He

cracks. 'Aaaaaagh,' he screams. He charges at me with hands held out like claws.

I run for it. I run down to my room and lock the door. Dad yells and shouts. He kicks and screams. But I lie low.

Tomorrow, when he calms down, I'll own up. I'll tell him how I went down the street and bought a new fly swat for fifty cents. I'll tell him about the currants and little bits of liquorice that I smeared on the fly swat.

I mean, I wouldn't really eat dead flies. Not unless it was for something important anyway.

The Incredible Henry McHugh

Robert Fisher

I am the Incredible Henry McHugh
you should see the things that I can do!
(and I'm only two)
I can . . .
tie laces in knots
spit peas into pots
squirt all the cream
and scream and SCREAM!

I can . . .
leave toys on the stair
pour honey in hair
scatter fried rice
play football with mice
sit down on the cat
be sick in a hat
slam the door, flood the floor,
and shout 'more, MORE, MORE!'

I can telephone Timbuctoo –
and frequently do,
hurl mud pies and rocks
put jelly in socks
pull Dracula faces
and stick Mum's pins in unlikely places.

I can . . .
pinch, poke, tickle and stroke,
wriggle, giggle, rattle and prattle,
scrawl on the wall
spill paint down the hall
pick heads off the flowers
dribble for hours
and when things go wrong
I just sing my song.

I'M not to blame.
You know my name,
I am Henry McHugh
the INCREDIBLE!
(I'm only two).

Horrible Harry and the Deadly Fish Tank

Suzy Kline

We have a fish tank in Room 2B. Last time Harry and I counted there were twenty-five fish swimming around in it.

Twenty guppies.

Four neon fish.

And one black molly.

Then there was horrible Monday. This is how it happened. Sidney came to school mad. He was mad about Harry putting ice water down his back on Friday.

Even his hair looked angry. It stood on end. Sidney probably didn't bother combing it.

Miss Mackle looked at the Monitor Chart. 'Boys and girls, I will announce the week's new monitors. Sidney is Messenger, Doug is Paper Monitor, Ida is Ant Monitor, Mary is Plant Monitor, Song Lee is Sweeper, and. . . .' When she finally got to Harry she said, 'Harry is Fish Monitor.'

Harry immediately got up and went back to feed the fish. He turned on the light in the tank and took roll. Carefully he recorded the number in the Fish Roll Book.

Then he checked the temperature. It was in the green part of the thermometer – in the 70–80 degree range.

At lunch time, Harry fed the fish and then lined up behind me in the cafeteria. 'I have my favourite dessert, Doug,' he said. 'Two pieces of Mum's home-made fudge. I'm saving it for us on the way home from school.'

I drooled. I knew how good Harry's mother's fudge was. Chocolate, nutty, and mmmmm good.

After lunch when we were working on maths, Harry walked back to check the tank. Then he shouted, 'The black molly is floating on the water. She's DEAD!'

Everyone rushed back to the tank.

Miss Mackle opened the cover of the tank and took out the net. She scooped up the dead fish. Then she put her finger in the water. 'Why, the water is hot! Someone has been fooling with the temperature knob.'

Everyone looked at the thermometer. The mercury was way above the green zone. 'Who would do such a horrible thing?' Miss Mackle exclaimed.

Everyone looked at Harry.

I did too. Harry loves to do horrible things.

Miss Mackle waited for someone to speak.

Sidney spoke first. 'Harry is the fish monitor. He did it!'

'Do you know anything about this?' Miss Mackle asked Harry.

Harry shook his head.

Miss Mackle said we wouldn't be doing 'little theatre' that afternoon. She didn't feel like doing anything fun. She was too disappointed.

We just worked at our seats the rest of the afternoon.

It was a long day.

When Harry lined up at three o'clock, no one wanted to stand next to him.

Except me.

'Do you think I did it?' Harry asked as we walked home.

I didn't say anything. I wasn't sure.

'Doug,' Harry said. 'I wouldn't do anything *that* horrible. I plan on being a great scientist someday. With you, remember? I would never take the life of a single living thing. Not a beetle, or an ant, or a single blade of grass.'

I knew Harry never mowed the lawn. He told his mother he couldn't kill the grass.

We walked home without talking. We didn't even eat Harry's home-made fudge. We just didn't feel like it. The next morning, Harry made a poster and put it up by the fish tank. It was a picture of a tombstone and a graveyard. It said GOD BLESS R BLAK MOLLY.

Then in the top part was a bunch of fish with yellow wings and haloes flying around.

'What's that up there?' I asked.

'Fish heaven,' Harry replied.

Miss Mackle started the morning as usual with a conversation.

'Boys and girls, we need to talk about our fish. We are responsible for them. Somehow, we made an error.'

Sidney raised his hand. 'Harry is the fish monitor. He likes to do horrible things. Harry did it. He should stay after school.' Then he sat back in his chair and smiled.

I looked at Sidney. Then it dawned on me. Revenge. That's what Sidney wanted! He wanted to get even because Harry had put ice water down his back.

Harry raised his fist at Sidney. 'I wouldn't cook a fish like that.'

'Prove it!' Sidney replied.

'Harry,' Miss Mackle said, 'do you know anything about how the black molly died?'

Harry shook his head.

Everyone made a face. No one believed Harry but me.

'Did anyone see someone at the fish tank just before the lunch bell?' I asked.

Song Lee had her hand in the air for the *first* time.

'Yes, Song Lee,' Miss Mackle said. 'Did you see someone?'

Softly, Song Lee spoke, 'I see Sidney by the tank just before bell ring. He reach behind where knob is.'

Sidney sank down in his chair.

Miss Mackle glared at him.

Sidney looked at the teacher, then the class. His face turned red. 'I didn't mean to kill the fish. I just . . . just . . .'

'Just what?' Miss Mackle asked.

'. . . wanted to get . . .' Sidney's voice got softer and softer '. . . Harry in trouble.'

'We'll talk about it after school,' Miss Mackle said firmly.

Holiday with the Fiend

Sheila Lavelle

The trouble with Angela is that she very easily gets bored. She's not content to read a book or paint a picture or knit herself a scarf. She has to be plotting and scheming and causing trouble all the time, and the more people she can find to play her tricks on, the better she likes it.

A holiday boarding house is a great place for somebody like Angela, and she didn't waste a single chance. She put big black plastic spiders in all the bathrooms, and frightened the two lady schoolteachers out of their wits. She pinched all the room keys off the board in the hall and muddled the numbers up before hanging them back on the wrong hooks. And one night she even crept into the larder while everybody was asleep and changed all the labels round on the boxes and tins of food. So there was salt in the sugar container and flour in the rice jar and peaches in the tins labelled baked beans. It made some of the meals a bit of a surprise, I can tell you.

I kept on refusing to have anything to do with her plans, and finally she stopped pestering me to help her and just got on with it herself. I was relieved not to be getting into trouble, but at the same time I couldn't help feeling a bit glum that I was missing all the excitement. It doesn't seem fair that the wicked people in the world have all the fun.

One morning Daniel and I came back from our early walk and caught her sneaking out of the dining room with one of her dad's muddy hiking boots on the end of a long pole. I stared at her in astonishment, and Daniel growled at

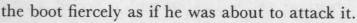

the boot fiercely as if he was about to attack it.

'Shurrup, you stupid dog,' hissed Angela. 'You'll wake everybody up.' And she shoved the boot into a carrier bag and hurried away upstairs.

I peered round the door into the dining room but I couldn't see what she had been up to. I didn't find out until we were all sitting at breakfast and Angela kept giggling so much she could hardly eat her scrambled eggs on toast.

'Look at the ceiling,' she whispered, when I begged her to tell me what was going on. I glanced upwards, and I almost choked.

Right across the white-painted ceiling from the doorway to the window were great big black muddy footprints. I looked fearfully at Mrs Down, but she was serenely serving coffee and fluttering her eyelashes at my dad.

'The rules say no muddy boots on the carpets,' murmured Angela slyly. 'They say nothing about the ceiling, do they?' She gave her tinkly little laugh. 'I bet you anything you like that nobody notices,' she said. 'People just don't look at ceilings.'

And do you know, she was right. I sat there fiddling nervously with my breakfast expecting that any minute somebody would give a shout. But not one person even glanced upwards, not during that breakfast or at any other meal for the rest of our holiday. As far as I know those muddy footprints are there to this day.

Snake in the Grass

Helen Cresswell

Robin could tell, right from the beginning, that he was going to enjoy the picnic. To begin with, Uncle Joe and Aunty Joy had brought him a present, a bugle.

He took a long, testing blow. The note went on and on and on – and on. He saw Aunty Joy shudder and his cousin Nigel put his hands to his ears. Nigel was twelve, and Robin hardly even came up to his shoulder.

'We'll be off now,' Uncle Joe said, climbing into his car. 'See you there.'

Robin got into the back seat of his father's car.

'It's lovely at Miller's Beck,' his mother said. 'You'll love it, Robin.'

Robin did not reply. The picnic hamper was on the back seat, too, and he was trying to squint between the wickerwork to see what was in there. In the end he gave up squinting and sniffed. Ham, was it? Tomatoes? Oranges, definitely, and was it – could it be – strawberries?

He sat back and began to practise the bugle. He kept playing the same three notes over and over again, and watched the back of his father's neck turning a dark red.

'D'ye *have* to play that thing now?' he growled at last. 'We shall all end up in a ditch!'

'I'm only trying to learn it, Dad,' said Robin. 'I've always wanted a bugle.'

An hour later, when they reached Miller's Beck, he had invented a tune that he really liked and had already played it about a hundred times. It was a kind of cross between 'Onward Christian Soldiers' and 'My Old Man's a Dustman'.

The minute the car stopped, Robin got out and ran down to the stream. He pulled off his shoes and socks and paddled in. The water was icy cold and clear as tap water, running over stones and gravel and small boulders.

Robin began to paddle downstream after a piece of floating bark he wanted for a boat, when:

'Ooooooooch!' he yelled. 'Owwwwwwch!'

A sharp pain ran through his foot. He balanced on one leg and lifted the hurt foot out of the water. He could see blood dripping from it.

'Oooooowh!' he yelled again. 'Help!'

He began to sway round and round on his good leg, like a spinning top winding down. He threw out his arms, yelled again and was down, flat on his bottom in the icy beck.

'Robin,' he heard his father scream. 'Robin.'

He sat where he was with the water above his waist and the hurt foot lifted above the water, still dripping blood. He couldn't even feel the foot any more. He just sat and stared at it as if it belonged to someone else.

His father was pulling off his shoes and socks and next minute was splashing in beside him and had lifted him clean up out of the water. Robin clutched him hard and water squelched between them. Robin's elbow moved sharply and he heard his father's yell.

'Hey, my glasses.'

Robin twisted his head and saw first that he was dripping blood all over his father's trousers, second that the bottoms of his father's trousers were in the water because he hadn't had time to roll them up, and third that lying at the bottom of the beck were his father's spectacles. Robin could see at a glance that they were broken – at least, one of the lenses was.

His father staggered blindly out of the water, smack into Uncle Joe, who was hopping on the bank.

'Here! Take him!' he gasped.

Then Robin was in Uncle Joe's arms, dripping blood and water all over *him*, and was carried back up the slope with his mother and Aunty Joy dancing and exclaiming around them.

It was half an hour before the picnic could really begin. By then, Robin was sitting on one of the folding chairs with his foot resting on a cushion on the other chair. This meant that both his parents were sitting on the grass. Robin's foot was bandaged with his father's handkerchief and the blood had soaked right through it and had made a great stain on the yellow cushion. Robin's shorts were hanging over the car bumper, where they were dripping on to Nigel's comic; Robin was wearing his swimming trunks and had his mother's new pink cardigan draped round his shoulders. There was blood on that, too.

Everyone's got a bit of blood, he noted with satisfaction.

Admittedly, his father and Uncle Joe had come off worst. His father sat half on the rug and half off with his trousers dripping. He had to keep squinting about him and twisting his head round to see through the one remaining lens of his glasses. Robin kept staring at him, thinking how queer he looked with one small squinting eye and one familiar large one behind the thick pebble lens. It made him look a different person – more a creature than a person, really, like something come up from under the sea.

'Are you comfy, dear?' asked his mother.

Robin nodded.

'Are you hungry?'

Robin nodded.

'Ravenous.'

'Pass Robin a sandwich, Nigel!' said Aunty Joy sharply. 'Sitting there stuffing yourself! And you'd better not have any more till we see how many Robin wants. Bless his heart! Does he look pale to you, Myra?'

The picnic got better and better every minute. Robin had at least three times his share of strawberries, and Aunty Joy made Nigel give Robin

his bag of crisps because she caught him sticking out his tongue at Robin. Nigel went off in a huff and found blood all over his comic and the minute he tried to turn the first page, it tore right across.

'That hanky's nearly soaked,' Robin said, watching Aunty Joy helping herself to the last of the strawberries. 'I've never seen so much blood. You should have seen it dripping into the water. It turned the whole stream a sort of horrible streaky red.'

Aunty Joy carried on spooning.

'If I'd been in the sea, I expect it'd have turned the whole *sea* red,' Robin went on. 'It was the thickest blood I ever saw. Sticky, thicky red blood – streams of it. Gallons. I bet it's killed all the fishes.'

Aunty Joy gulped and bravely spooned out the remaining juice.

'I won't bleed to death, will I?' he went on. 'Bleed and bleed and bleed till there isn't another drop of blood left in my whole body, and I'm dead. Just like an empty bag, I'd be.'

Aunty Joy turned pale and put down her spoon.

'Just an empty bag of skin,' repeated Robin thoughtfully. 'That's what I'll be.'

'Of course you won't, darling!' cried his mother.

'Well, this handkerchief certainly is bloody,' said Robin. 'There must've been a bucket of blood. A *bowlful* anyway!'

Aunty Joy pushed away her bowl of strawberries.

'I wonder what it could've been?' went on Robin. 'That cut me, I mean.'

'Glass!' his mother said. 'It must have been. It's disgraceful, leaving broken glass lying about like that. Someone might have been crippled for life.'

'Dad,' said Robin, after a pause. At first his father did not hear. He had stretched out at full length and was peering closely at his newspaper with his one pebble eye.

'Dad!' His father looked up. 'Dad, hadn't you better go and pick *your* glass up? From your specs, I mean? Somebody else might go and cut themselves.'

'The child's right!' his mother cried. 'Fancy the angel thinking of that! Off you go, George, and pick it up, straight away!'

Robin's father got up slowly. His trousers flapped wetly about his legs and his bloodstained shirt clung to him.

'And mind you pick up every little bit!' she called after him. 'Don't you want those strawberries, Joy?'

She shook her head.

'Could you manage them, Robin?'

Robin could. He did. When he had finished, he licked the bowl.

Once the tea things were cleared away, everyone settled down. Aunty Joy was knitting a complicated lacy jacket that meant she had to keep counting under her breath. His mother read, Uncle Joe decided to wash his car, and his father was searching for the sports pages of his newspaper that had blown away while he was down at the beck picking up his broken spectacles. Nigel had a new model yacht and took it down to the stream. Robin watched him go. All *he* had was a sodden comic and the bugle.

He played the bugle until the back of his father's neck was crimson again and Aunty Joy had twice lost count of her stitches and had to go right back to the beginning of the row again. For a change, he tried letting her get halfway across a row and then, without warning, gave a deafening blast. She jumped, the needles jerked, and half the stitches came off.

After the third time, even that didn't seem funny any more. Robin swung his legs down and tested the bad foot. Surprisingly, it hardly hurt at all. He stood right up and took a few steps. His mother looked up.

'Robin!' she squealed. 'Darling! What are you doing?'

'It's all right, Mum,' he said. 'It doesn't hurt. It's stopped bleeding now. It looks worse than it is, the handkerchief being all bloody.'

'I really think you should sit still,' she said.

Robin took no notice and went limping down to the beck. Nigel was in midstream, turning his yacht. It was a beauty.

'Swap you it for my bugle,' he said, after a time.

'What?' Nigel turned to face him. 'You're crazy. Crazy little kid!'

'I'll swap,' repeated Robin.

'Well, I *won't*.' Nigel turned his back again.

Robin stayed where he was. Lying by his feet were Nigel's shoes, with the socks stuffed inside them. Gently, using the big toe of his bandaged foot, he edged them off the bank and into the water. They lay there, the shoes filled and the socks began to balloon and sway. Fascinated, Robin watched. At last the socks, with a final graceful swirl, drifted free of the shoes and began to float downstream.

Robin watched them out of sight. After that, there seemed nothing he could do. What *could* you do, with your foot all bandaged up? The picnic was going all to pieces.

He felt a little sting on his good leg and looked down in time to see a gnat making off. He swatted hard at it, and with a sudden inspiration clapped a hand to his leg, fell to his knees and let out a bloodcurdling howl.

'Robin!' He heard his mother scream. 'Robin!'

They were thundering down the slope towards him now, all of them, even Uncle Joe, wash-leather in hand.

'Darling! What is it?'

'Snake!' gasped Robin, squeezing his leg tight with his fingers.

'Where?' cried Aunty Joy. He pointed upstream, towards the long grass. He noticed that her wool was wound round her waist and her knitting trailing behind her, both needles missing.

'Where did it *bite* you?' she cried.

Robin took his hands away from the leg. Where they had clutched it, the skin was red and in the middle of the crimson patch was the tiny prick made by the gnat.

'Ooooooh!' he heard his mother give an odd, sighing moan and looked up in time to see that she was falling. His father leapt forward and caught her just in time and they both fell to the ground together.

Biting the dust, thought Robin, watching them.

'Here!' cried Aunty Joy. 'We'll have to suck the poison out!'

She dropped to her knees beside him, her hair awry and face flushed. Next minute she had her mouth to Robin's leg and was sucking it, with fierce, noisy sucks. He tried to jerk his leg away but she had it in an iron grip. At last she stopped sucking and turning her head aside spat fiercely right into the stream. It was almost worth having her suck, to see her spit.

'Carry him up to the car!' she gasped, scrambling up. 'I must see to Myra!'

Uncle Joe picked him up for the second time that day and carried him away. Over his shoulder Robin could see the others bending over his mother, trying to lift her. Best of all, he could see Nigel beating round in the long grass with a stick while his boat, forgotten, sailed slowly off downstream.

Gone, Robin thought. Gone for ever.

Uncle Joe put him down in the driving seat of his own car.

'Be all right for a minute, old chap?' he asked.

Robin nodded.

'Have a mint.' He fished for one from his pocket. 'Back in a minute. Better go and see if I can find that brute of a snake. Don't want Nigel bitten.'

Then he was gone. Robin stared through the windscreen towards the excited huddle by the bank. It seemed to him that everyone was having a good time except himself. There he sat, quite alone, scratching absently at the gnat bite.

Idly he looked about the inside of the car. Usually he wasn't allowed in. It was Uncle Joe's pride and joy. The dashboard glittered with knobs and dials. He twiddled one or two of them, and got the radio working, then a green light on, then a red, then the windscreen wipers working. He pushed the gearstick and it slotted smoothly into place. To his left, between the bucket seats, was the handbrake. He knew how to release it – his father had shown him.

The brake was tightly on, and it was a struggle. He was red in the face and panting by the time he sat upright again. The car was rolling forward, very gently, down the grassy slope,

then gathering speed as it approached the beck.

By the time they saw him it was too late. The car lurched, then bounced off the bank and into the water. It stopped, right in midstream.

Robin looked out and saw himself surrounded by water.

The captain goes down with his ship! he thought.

He saw his mother sit up, stare, then fall straight back again. He saw the others, wet, bloodstained and horror-struck, advancing towards him.

With a sigh he let his hands fall from the wheel. It was the end of the picnic, he could see that. He wound down the window and put out a hand to wave. Instead, it met glass and warm flesh. He heard a splash and a tinkle. Level with the window, he saw his father's face. Now *both* his eyes were small and squinting. Small, squinting and murderous.

The picnic was definitely over.

Jelly Jake and Butter Bill

Leroy F Jackson

Jelly Jake and Butter Bill
One dark night when all was still
Pattered down the long, dark stair,
And no one saw the guilty pair;
Pushed aside the pantry door

And there found everything galore –
Honey, raisins, orange-peel,
Cold chicken aplenty for a meal,
Gingerbread enough to fill
Two such boys as Jake and Bill.

Well, they ate and ate and ate,
Gobbled at an awful rate
Till I'm sure they soon weighed more
Than double what they did before.
And then, it's awful, still it's true,
The floor gave way and they went through.

Filled so full they couldn't fight,
Slowly they sank out of sight.
Father, Mother, Cousin Ann,
Cook and nurse and furnace man
Fished in forty-dozen ways
After them, for twenty days;

But not a soul has chanced to get
A glimpse or glimmer of them yet.
And I'm afraid we never will —
Poor Jelly Jake and Butter Bill.

When I Lived Down Cuckoo Lane and Lost a Fox Fur, and a Lot More Besides

Jean Wills

'Next Saturday your aunts are coming to tea.'

I grinned at Mum, and she smiled at me.

The town aunts were good news. I could dress up in their clothes. Mum would have a good gossip. And we'd all enjoy a tremendous feast.

I asked if my best friend could come as well.

'As long as you're not noisy.'

'Noisy? *US?*'

I went and wrote a message and put it in the cricket post.

SATERDAY ARENTS DRESSING UP

It was our favourite game just then. We'd been mothers. Grandmothers. Queens and princesses. But never aunts. And the town aunts were really fancy dressers.

Next time I looked in the wall there was another message.

I looked up at the sky, and Pat and Mick ran out of the alley and captured me.

'So that's what they do with that wall,' Mick said.

The cricket post was a secret no longer.

Pat stopped whistling through his gap. ' "Cuming Sat God"?'

' "Cuming" is coming. "Sat" could be Saturday. And "God" is good,' said Mick. 'Amen.'

They both turned to me.

'What is happening on Saturday?'

I wouldn't tell them anything. My best friend and I were going to have the town aunts all to ourselves.

On Saturday afternoon we hid behind the wall to wait. We waited and waited.

'Suppose they don't come?' my best friend said.

'They're always late. They have to dress up, go to the shops, and catch the train. And the Number 5 bus. They'll come.'

Later on two people turned the corner, one short, one tall.

'It's them!'

'At last.' We started out, but my best friend stopped. 'You didn't say there'd be dogs.'

'What dogs?'

'The ones they're carrying.'

'They're furs. I told you. The town aunts are fancy dressers.'

'And eaters, you said.'

'And eaters too.' I pointed to the parcels.

We started to run.

The town aunts opened their arms out wide. They kissed us, called us 'dear' and 'darling', and gave us their parcels to carry.

We made so much noise walking down Cuckoo Lane that people looked out of their windows to watch. Mrs Thresher came out and leaned on her gate. The town aunts laughed, and swept into our house.

Leaving the parcels on the kitchen table we followed them upstairs.

Mum and Dad's bed was soon covered with coats. Hats. Gloves. Furs. The town aunts kicked off their high-heeled shoes. They patted their hair, and powdered their noses. The room was full of a lovely scent.

Then down we all went to open the parcels.

There were chocolate fingers. Coconut cream. Brandy snaps. An iced cake and walnut whips.

Mum made tea in her best silver pot. The best china stood ready on the best silver tray. There were cucumber sandwiches, sausage rolls, and a Dundee cake, as well as everything else.

We packed our share of the feast in the cake

box. When Mum and the aunts were safely shut up we crept back upstairs to the bedroom.

'What shall we do first?' my best friend said. 'Eat or dress up?'

'Dress up.'

My best friend wasn't sure.

'Then we can have a whopping big feast afterwards. And eat the whole lot in one go.'

I put on my tall aunt's mauve silk coat. Her black straw hat. And the high-heeled shoes.

'You do look funny,' my best friend said. 'Miss Baloni gone barmy.'

I didn't want to look like Miss Baloni, but my glamorous, exciting town aunt.

My best friend disappeared inside my short aunt's coat. She pulled on a hat like a chimney pot.

'*You* look like Green Hill.'

My best friend snatched up a chocolate finger.

'Not yet!'

'Why not?'

And that's when it all went wrong.

As I tottered forward to grab the cake box a cucumber sandwich flew out. My best friend trod on it and fell over. Clutching at the bed she pulled off a fox fur.

'Eurgh! I don't like it. Take it away!'

Instead I wriggled the fox fur towards her.

She climbed on to the dressing table. I threw

the fur, and she threw it back. It hit the window, and flopped on the ledge.

Outside somebody whistled.

'Did you see that?'

'It's not a cat.'

'Nor a dog.'

'Nor a rabbit.'

'It's a fox!'

My best friend climbed down. We crawled beneath the window. I reached up and wriggled the fox. And giggled. And wriggled. And the more I did the more I couldn't stop. And my best friend couldn't either. Until. . . .

The fur fell out of the window.

We got tangled up in the town aunts' coats. By the time we looked out Pat and Mick were in the alley, and the fox fur with them.

Downstairs a door opened. Shrieks of laughter blew up the stairs. Then Mum called.

'Are you two still up there?'

'Yes.'

'You're not to touch your aunts' things with your sticky fingers.'

If only that was all we had done!

'Go out into the garden.'

We laid the clothes back on the bed. Took the cake box, and ran downstairs.

Pat and Mick were in the alley, stroking the fox.

'Poor thing,' said Mick fiercely. 'How would you like it? Glass beads for eyes. Your insides out, and lined with silk.'

'It's not my fault,' I said.

'We'll bury it. That's what we'll do. Deep in the jungle, where nobody will ever find it.' Pat began whistling.

'You can't!' I said.

They walked away.

'I must have it back. I must, I must. I'll give you . . .'

'What?'

They stood at the top of the alley and waited. I held out the box. '. . . some of this.'

They took the whole lot, and ran off with it.

After we'd put the fox fur back we went to see how far Mum and the town aunts had got with their tea. All that talking and laughing. . . . There couldn't have been much time for eating.

But. . . .

My best friend stared, and so did I. The best china plates were covered in crumbs, nothing else!

As we walked to the bus stop with the town aunts Mrs Thresher leaned on her gate to watch. Windows opened. The fox furs bounced on the town aunts' chests.

'Did you have a lovely feed, my darlings?'

We couldn't speak, just nodded instead. And

tried not to think about sausage rolls. Coconut cream. Brandy snaps. Walnut whips. Iced cake. Chocolate fingers. Even a cucumber sandwich would have been something.

As they kissed us goodbye the air was full of their lovely scent. We waved goodbye, then walked back slowly.

'The rotten things,' my best friend said. 'The greedy, rotten things.'

The Teacher Trap

Martin Waddell

'Here it is!' said Harriet, plonking the Fruit Salad Anthea bowl on the end of the table in the Gym, where P7's Grand Feast was laid out.

P7 gathered round.

'What is it?' asked Fat Olga, standing well back from the placid green mixture in the bowl.

'It's a fruit salad!' said Anthea. 'Named after me.'

'Because she's my best friend,' said Harriet.

Anthea beamed proudly round at the rest of P7 who hadn't had fruit salads named after them because they weren't Harriet's Best Friends.

'What's *in* it?' said Sylvester Wise, going to the nub of the problem as usual.

'Lots of things!' said Anthea. 'Lots of lovely lovely things to match lovely lovely me!'

Not everybody present thought that Anthea was lovely, but nobody said so.

'It's smoky green, sort of,' said Olga, and she

considered *sniffing*, but thought better of it. You never know where a sniff will get you.

'Jolly well done, Harriet!' said Sylvester.

Harriet looked at him suspiciously. She was right to be suspicious. There was bound to be something wrong when the Leader of the Anti-Harriet League said something nice to Harriet.

'Brilliant, Harriet!' said Fat Olga, taking her cue from her Leader.

'Very nice,' said Marky Brown.

'Smashing!' said Charlie Green.

'You all sick, or something?' said Harriet. 'You don't *look* sick. Not any sicker than usual, that is.'

'Not at all, Harriet,' said Sylvester. 'It is our new policy. "Be-Nice-to-Harriet!" '

'Why?' said Harriet.

'It's because they really *like* you, Harriet, I expect,' said Anthea.

There was a long silence.

'Quite right!' said Sylvester, lying through his teeth.

'Prove it!' said Harriet.

'I will!' said Sylvester, and he walked down the table and whipped the cover off the ham sandwiches.

'I've named my ham sandwiches after you!' said Sylvester. 'That proves it!'

Harriet frowned. She wasn't sure that she

liked having ham sandwiches named after her.

'And my apple tart!' said Fat Olga, showing Harriet the apple tart.

'And my swiss roll!' said Charlie Green.

'I would have named my jelly after you, but I sat on it on the bus!' said Marky Brown, but he showed Harriet the sign and some bits of sat-on jelly.

The sign said: Jelly: Harriet.

'Oh lovely!' said Anthea. 'Aren't you proud to have all those things named after you, Harriet?'

Harriet looked at the Ham Sandwiches Harriet and the Apple Tart Harriet and the Swiss Roll Harriet and the empty plate where the sat-on Jelly Harriet would have been, if it hadn't been jelly-sat.

'Hmmm,' she said.

and

'Uhuh!'

and

'This needs thinking about!'

Harriet went away to think about it in the boiler room.

'Got her!' said Sylvester Wise triumphantly.

'Wise!' boomed Mr Tiger. 'Wise! Here, boy!'

Sylvester was out by the bike shed, counting bike rides on Charlie Green's bicycle, as the Anti-Harriet League lived up to their obligation to their voters.

'Sir?' said Sylvester.

'Who made what, Wise?' said Mr Tiger, coming to the point as usual. He wasn't the Pride of Slow Street for nothing, and he had been sent to find out, following an Emergency Meeting of the Staff in Miss Grandston's Room.

'*What* what, sir?' said Sylvester.

'The foodstuffs in the Grand Feast, Wise!' barked Mr Tiger. 'Who prepared what?'

'Don't know, sir,' said Sylvester innocently.

'Of course you know, boy!' said Mr Tiger. 'You're not foolish enough to eat anything made by Harriet, are you? Not after last year! The Staff *demand* to know what Harriet made, so that we can steer clear of it.'

'I couldn't say, sir,' said Sylvester.

Mr Tiger took a deep breath. 'There will no doubt be some particular foodstuff that you will *not* be touching, Wise?' he said, with tiger-like cunning.

'Oh yes, sir,' said Sylvester. 'The apple tart, sir. I wouldn't touch *that*, sir, not for anything!'

'Aah!' breathed Mr Tiger. 'Good boy, Wise! A wink is as good as a nod! Splendid little chap!'

And he rushed off to tell the Staff.

'What's wrong with my apple tart then?' said Fat Olga, coming up to Sylvester.

'Nothing,' said Sylvester.

'You told him you would be steering clear of the apple tart!' said Fat Olga.

'I'm allergic to apples,' said Sylvester.

'No you're not!' said Marky. 'You have one every breaktime!'

'I am *today*,' said Sylvester.

'I don't understand,' said Fat Olga.

'I didn't think you would,' said Sylvester. 'It's all part of my plan.'

'What plan?' said Olga.

'My Teacher Trap!' said Sylvester.

'No apple tart, anybody!' said Mr Tiger, marshalling the Staff.

'No apple tart!' the Staff chorused.

'And no ham sandwiches or swiss roll either!'

said Miss Granston.

'Why not?' said Mr Tiger.

'Because I've spied out the land!' said Miss Granston. 'They've got Harriet's name on!'

'Aaaaaaaah!' moaned the Staff.

And Miss Granston led them down the corridor toward the P7 Grand Feast with a proud beam of achievement on her face, little knowing what was to come.

'Anthea!' said Harriet. '*Look*, Anthea!'

'What, Harriet?' said Anthea, who was busy stuffing herself with little sausages on sticks, because she liked little sausages on sticks.

'My fruit salad!' said Harriet.

'*My* fruit salad, you mean,' said Anthea. 'Fruit Salad Anthea!'

'Yes,' said Harriet. 'It's the most popular thing there is!'

Harriet was right.

The teachers had gathered in a cloud round Fruit Salad Anthea. For one thing, it was at the far end of the table from Apple Tart Harriet and Jam Roll Harriet and even Ham Sandwiches Harriet, which made it a safer place to be, and for another it was delicious.

So it should have been, with apples and oranges and pineapples and peaches and cherries and grapes and avocados and invigorating nonalcoholic nettle wine and elderberry and nutmeg and cherry, with half a bottle of raw artichokes on top. 'Delicious!' said Miss Tremloe, sipping from her spoon.

'Do have some more, Mr Tiger!' said Miss Granston, and she helped her right-hand man to a fourth serving.

'Spot on!' said Mr Cousins. 'I feel quite out of myself.'

'. . . Om . . . pom . . . pom!' giggled Miss Wilson.

'Really lovely concoction, Anthea!' said Mrs Whitten, spooning away. 'Do congratulate your mother . . .'

'It wasn't *my* mother, Miss,' said Anthea. 'It's just named after me. It was . . .'

But her voice was drowned out by the sound coming from the corner where Miss Ash, who had had one or two helpings too many of the delicious fruit salad, was showing Mrs Barton how to do a Two-Step.

'One-two-three, one-two-three!' cried Miss Ash, adding a step too many because she suddenly felt carefree and happy and generous.

'Music! We need music!' cried Miss Wilson, flinging her arms in the air, and beginning to twirl, a wild glow lighting up her cheeks.

Miss Tremloe, who taught music and movement, was not to be outdone. She grabbed her guitar and strummed.

It was a fierce strumming, a jungle beat, something to do with fruit juices and invigorating wine.

Miss Wilson whipped off her shoes and grabbed Mr Cousins, who thought his lucky day had come.

They waltzed around the floor. Mr Tiger, caught up in the spirit of the thing, abandoned his pipe and his fourth helping of fruit salad and grabbed Miss Granston by the elbow. Off they clipped, to a Military Two-Step.

Mrs Barton did a Fandango with Mrs Whitten, followed by a strange and exotic dance she had once seen in a night club in Benidorm on a blind date. Hair was let loose, legs and arms flew. All the teachers were dancing and singing and bopping about to the throb of Miss Tremloe's unchained guitar.

'OOOOOH!' said Olga.

'Mission accomplished!' said Sylvester, with great satisfaction.

'They're all . . .' began Charlie Green, but he didn't get finished, because Mrs Barton grabbed him by the wrist, and whirled him into the dance.

It was then that Miss Wilson sat down on the floor.

She did it suddenly, because she had been

showing Mr Cousins what the Leading Swan did in Act Three of 'Swan Lake', and somehow the swan legs had done a wobble.

'Oooooh!' moaned Miss Wilson.

CRASH! Mr Tiger and Miss Granston fell over her.

BANG! Mrs Barton followed suit.

WALLOP!

The wallop was Mrs Whitten, who had retreated to a stool but fell off it just the same, bringing an abrupt end to Mrs Barton's dance.

All the teachers lay on the floor.

None of them stirred.

The P1s and P2s and P3s and P4s and P5s and P6s stood very still, and looked frightened.

The P7s cheered!

And that was when Sylvester Wise showed his true leadership qualities again.

'Silence, everyone!' he cried. 'Do not disturb our sleeping teachers! All Junior Classes will return to their rooms, collect their coats and bags and fly away home!'

Everybody cleared off, except the P7s.

'What about us?' said Charlie.

'We've still got the apple tart and the swiss roll and the ham sandwiches to finish,' said Sylvester. 'Nobody touched them!'

'You did that deliberately, Sylvester Wise!' said Harriet.

'Did what?' said Sylvester, tucking into the feast.

'You fixed it so the teachers would all stick to my fruit salad,' said Harriet.

'Didn't you want them to take it?' said Sylvester.

'Yes, but not so *much* of it,' said Harriet, who was beginning to wonder about the effects of nonalcoholic nettle wine and elderberry and nutmeg and cherry, with half a bottle of artichoke, all mixed in with fruit.

'They're all laid out on the floor, Harriet,' said Anthea.

'And that's where we're leaving them!' said Sylvester. 'It was *your* fruit salad, you can sort it out with them, when they come round!'

The rest of P7 cleared off, leaving Harriet and Anthea and a pile of teachers in the middle of the floor.

'I think . . . I think we're in trouble again, Harriet,' said Anthea unhappily.

Acknowledgements

The compiler and publishers wish to thank the following for permission to use copyright material in this anthology:

Lance Salway for 'The Boy Who Wasn't Bad Enough'.

Abelard-Schuman for 'Playing With Cuthbert' by René Goscinny from *Nicholas and the Gang*.

Viking Kestrel for 'The Crooked Little Finger' by Philippa Pearce from *Lion at School*.

Penguin Books Australia Limited for 'Licked' by Paul Jennings from *Unbearable*.

Faber & Faber for 'The Incredible Henry McHugh' by Robert Fisher from *Funny Folk*.

Viking for 'Horrible Harry and the Deadly Fish Tank' by Suzy Kline from *Horrible Harry and the Ant Invasion*.

Hamish Hamilton for 'Holiday With the Fiend' by Sheila Lavelle from *Holiday With the Fiend*.

Helen Cresswell for 'Snake in the Grass' from *Baker's Dozen*.

Mrs Ruth Jackson for 'Jelly Jake and Butter Bill' by Leroy F Jackson from *The Peter Patter Book*.

Andersen Press for 'When I Lived Down Cuckoo Lane and Lost a Fox Fur, and a Lot More Besides' by Jean Wills from *When I Lived Down Cuckoo Lane*.

Blackie and Co. for 'The Teacher Trap' by Martin Waddell from *Harriet and the Flying Teachers*.

Join the RED FOX Reader's Club

The Red Fox Reader's Club is for readers of all ages. All you have to do is ask your local bookseller or librarian for a Red Fox Reader's Club card. As an official Red Fox Reader you only have to borrow or buy eight Red Fox books in order to qualify for your own Red Fox Reader's Clubpack – full of exciting surprises! If you have any difficulty obtaining a Red Fox Reader's Club card please write to: Random House Children's Books Marketing Department, 20 Vauxhall Bridge Road, London SW1V 2SA.